FIREBIRD

ELIZABETH WEIN

Barrington Stoke

For Sara. You know all the reasons why.

First published in 2018 in Great Britain by
Barrington Stoke Ltd
18 Walker Street, Edinburgh, EH3 7LP

www.barringtonstoke.co.uk

Text © 2018 Elizabeth Gatland

A CIP catalogue record for this book is available from the British Library upon request

ISBN: 978-1-78112-831-2

Printed in China by Leo

Contents

PROLOGUE

I am not a traitor.

I have been asked to defend myself to this tribunal, and I am going to do so plainly. I will speak of things that are now forbidden, for which I ask your pardon. Nothing I say will go beyond these walls.

I am Anastasia Viktorovna Nabokova. Anastasia is the name of a saint, Anastasia the Healer. Anastasia was also an empress, the first wife of Czar Ivan the Terrible. And it is the name of the youngest of the four murdered daughters of Nicholas II, the Russian empire's last Romanov czar. I don't think our glorious leader Stalin would approve of the name Anastasia. It is a holy name and a royal name, and we are no longer supposed to worship the saints and the czars and the Romanovs. Those are relics of Imperial Russia, and they died when the Soviet Union was born.

But Anastasia means resurrection – rebirth. I think it is a good name for a girl who is fighting to save her nation from an invading army.

That is what I am doing.

I am not holy, nor am I royal, and everyone calls me Nastia because it is shorter. But I am still proud of my name. Nastia is not the name of a traitor.

It is true I landed my plane behind enemy lines. I am a pilot in the Soviet Air Force, and I landed my Soviet Yak-1 fighter aircraft in territory held by the German fascists. I risked them taking my plane and learning specialist secrets of our country's top aircraft engineers. I also risked being taken prisoner myself and being tortured for information about our air force.

In any case, I accept that I took this risk and that perhaps I did not act with full responsibility.

Stalin's Order Number 227 of July 1942 forbids us to retreat. If we do, or if we allow ourselves to be taken prisoner by the enemy, we are considered guilty of treason and will be shot. The order tells us: *Not one step back!* We shout this to each other for encouragement. And we whisper it to ourselves between combat missions – in the brief hours when we are able to rest. *Not one step back!*

But any act of cowardice might be a step back. Any mistake could get you shot.

It is true that I am not the same person I was before the war. But I am not a coward, I am not a traitor, and I did not run away.

Let me tell you how I became a pilot and why I landed my plane behind enemy lines – and what I did afterwards.

And then you can judge for yourself.

PART 1: EARLY SUMMER, 1941

Leningrad, on the ground

CHAPTER 1

It was June. It was a sunny day and it was my afternoon off. That was the day the war started.

I was on the Neva River, where it flows through the city of Leningrad, past apartment buildings and colourful church domes. I shouted instructions at my rowing club team as we sat in our eight-man boat.

I had finished high school and was working as a full-time instructor at the Leningrad Youth Aeroclub. I lived at the aeroclub now – this was my first job away from home. I had a salary and my own bunk in the clubhouse and an instructor's uniform. I took most of my meals there, except once a week when I visited my parents. Other girls flew at the aeroclub as students, but I was the only woman who worked there, apart from the Chief Flight Instructor.

The other young instructors, all boys, became my friends. Most of us had been in school together but not all in the same year group. Eight of these boys were in the First Neva Rowing Club. They were training to qualify for the regional championships, and because I am not very big they asked me to be their cox. I thought I would like going along in their boat – steering and telling these eight big boys what to do. I was flattered that they thought I could make sure they were safe on the river. So I said yes.

On the day the war started, I was crouched in the stern of our boat as usual. The rudder strings were in my hands as I faced my crew. We were all fully focused on shaving a few seconds off our current racing speed.

I shouted at them: "Next – stroke. Full – pressure. In – three. In – two. In—"

I broke off in the middle of the countdown. I'd heard something.

The boys kept rowing. I hadn't told them to stop.

Without me yelling at them, the only sounds were the creak of the seats in the boat, the splash of water and the crew's grunts of effort.

But now they could all hear the noise that had stopped me in the middle of my command.

It was an announcement being broadcast on the city's loudspeakers. We couldn't make out the words, but there was a frightening urgency in the tinny ring of the announcer's tone.

The boys at the oars heard it too.

Big Stefan, our reliable stroke, was sitting facing me. He was the oarsman who had to set the rhythm for the team. Stefan gave me a concerned, questioning frown.

I shouted, "Hold her up!"

The crew reacted with practised control. They stopped rowing at once and feathered their oars as one machine – not eight individual men. But I was too intent on listening to the broadcast to take pride in their smoothness. We glided on the water as the boat slowed down.

We all had our heads raised, staring at the sky as if we might see an answer there. We strained to hear the words of the loudspeaker as it blared the announcement out across the city.

Big Stefan was always slow to get excited, but even he turned his head away from me to look backwards. So did everybody else. Now we could all see what was ahead of us.

"Sounds like an emergency," Andrei said. He liked to know what was going on at all times. "A train wreck, maybe?"

"No ..." Ivan replied. He was a worrier.

"No," I repeated.

My crew all looked back towards me, waiting for a command. Their oars were still feathered in the water, and the boat had nearly slowed to a halt. Soon we'd start drifting downstream if I didn't give them another order. I was the one who told them what to do. They trusted me.

I knew we were all thinking the same thing, but the eight boys were waiting for me to say it out loud.

So I did.

"We are at war."

I didn't need to shout at them the way I did when we were rowing. I didn't need to raise my voice at all, because my team were all silent now, and still – a strange moment of calm in the June sunlight with the water of the Neva flowing over their oars.

Everything was about to change.

"We are at war with Germany," I said calmly, and I was amazed to hear myself saying these words. It seemed as if I had been waiting all my life to say them.

"*We're finally at war.*"

CHAPTER 2

I was born in a nation at war. I grew up in the shadow of war. And, like everyone else my own age, I had been waiting all my life for "the future war".

My father met my mother when he was shot in the knee in the 1917 October Revolution. She dragged him off the street to safety – just a young city girl doing a kindness to a stranger. Later, my mother joined my father as a Red Army volunteer.

They were married very quickly, but while they were soldiers in the Civil War they hardly saw each other. My mother was a spy, carrying secret messages. Later, she also carried her baby daughter – me – cuddled in a sling on her tummy. Before a mission, she'd rub salt in the corners and secret places of my small body, until my soft baby skin grew angry and red. I'd scream and scream, and then my mother would get past the authorities by pretending she was looking for a doctor for her baby's rash.

I don't remember that. But I also don't remember the first time I stood on a pair of skis or held a gun. You see, before I could talk or walk I was already a loyal Red Army fighter. I was *born* to fight for the Motherland.

In the year after my parents' marriage, my father helped to finish off the Romanov Empire so that our glorious Motherland could become the Soviet Union. He was one of the team who executed Czar Nicholas II and his wife and children. He drove the truck that carried their bodies away.

Our glorious leader, Stalin, has now ruled that we must never again speak of the Romanovs and their shameful deaths. But I can't help thinking about them, because I believe my father was affected by his involvement in the removal of the Romanovs for the rest of his life.

When the Revolution began in 1917, and the Czar's family were first imprisoned in their home at the Alexander Palace, they all thought they'd manage to escape somehow. Czar Nicholas II's daughters, Olga and Tatiana and Marie and Anastasia Romanova, hid jewels in their underwear. That way they'd have something valuable to take with them if they ever managed to get out of Russia. The girls kept those jewels close against their skin, even when they were exiled to Siberia. And when they were lined up to be shot during the panic of the Civil War, some of the bullets hit the hidden diamonds and bounced off their bodies like hail. The bullets didn't kill them, so the executioners had to stab them with bayonets. That's how their secret jewels were discovered. Afterwards, my father and the executioners took back the diamonds for the state.

When the Civil War was over, my father became a curator at the Alexander Palace Museum – the very place where the Czar and his family had lived before the Revolution.

He would tell me, "It's important to remember the history of the old nation while making a new one, my Nastia. That's why you're named Anastasia – meaning rebirth. An old name for a new generation."

My father had helped to destroy the Russian Empire, and now he needed to preserve its memory for his daughter's generation to learn from. To help us prepare for the next war – the future war. The war that *my* generation would have to fight.

We didn't know exactly who we would be fighting. But we knew that a war would come. We guessed it would be with Germany. Before the Revolution, the Germans had killed millions of Russian soldiers in the Great War. Now their new leader, Hitler, was itching to gobble up Europe. And so, while I was growing up, our Red Army prepared for this future war by fighting in China, in Spain and in Finland. Along with all my school friends, I joined exciting clubs where we learned to shoot rifles and jump with parachutes. Some of us, such as the members of the First Neva Rowing Club, learned to fly.

I was *ready* for this war.

We were *all* ready.

★

On that sunny June day on the Neva River, we rowed back to the boathouse. I told my crew what to do as usual. My normal, familiar rowing commands were the only words spoken the whole way back.

We all changed out of our rowing gear and back into our street clothes, then gathered at the boathouse entrance.

"Where do you think they're recruiting, Nastia?" Andrei asked.

Everybody looked at me. They knew my mother worked as a secretary in the NKVD, the police organisation which rounded up anyone suspected of treachery against the state or against our glorious leader, Josef Stalin. My friends assumed that if anybody knew where to sign up to fight, it would be me.

The faces of my friends were serious, but I could tell by their eyes that they were as excited and nervous as I was.

"The Komsomol Office," I guessed, replying to Andrei's question. Our aeroclub, our rowing club and every other out-of-school activity I knew were all run by the Komsomol – the young people's branch of the Communist Party. "They get information direct from the capital in Moscow."

"Let's go together," Big Stefan said, as calm as always and setting the pace for his team. "We're pilots. Better than that – we're flight instructors. Maybe if we sign up together they'll send us to the same air force regiment."

CHAPTER 3

Going to the Komsomol Office together was a good idea in theory.

We had to take a train, which was packed with tense young people, all doing the same thing. Most of us were subdued, as we didn't know what to expect when we got there. But we could hear a group of boys further down the carriage having a heated argument about how the war had started.

"We had a pact with Germany!" one of the boys said. "A peace treaty! How dare they attack us?"

"You know they were never going to stick to the treaty," another boy replied. "That fascist Hitler has invaded just about every country in Europe!"

"Well, we're ready for those fascists," the first boy exclaimed. "I'm the best sharp-shooter in my class!"

The train was stifling in the summer heat. I could feel sweat running down my back as we lurched over the rails.

Ivan, our rowing team's worrier, wiped his own face and frowned. "I hope the Red Army has plenty of guns to go around."

I admit that I wondered the same thing when we got to the Komsomol Office itself. The grey concrete building was overrun with high-school and university students, girls as well as boys, all clamouring to join the Red Army so they could fight against Germany. There was a crush of people around the front door, with a long queue trailing into the street.

"We should have worn our aeroclub uniforms," Ivan said as we tried to get closer to the door. "Then they'd take us more seriously."

"We're *pilots*," Big Stefan said with firm confidence. "We're not high-school kids. Forget about waiting in line. Come on. Let's pull rank."

Big Stefan's plan worked. We stayed in a tough tight group. Nine flight instructors had definite priority over a crowd of teens who'd earned their rifle badges or tried out a couple of parachute jumps.

Pretty soon we managed to sign up for an appointment with a recruiter. Then we had to sit and wait on a bench in a dark, windowless passage across from a group of students. They were about our own age and from the Physics Department at Leningrad State University. The Komsomol official sitting in a smoky office behind a closed door seemed to be calling them in one by one.

"We'll go in together," Big Stefan insisted. "They'll be wasting time talking to us one by one if we're all going to end up in the same place."

"Good idea," Andrei said with enthusiasm. He seemed glad to have a plan.

One of the physics students leaning against the wall asked lightly, "What are you, a tank-driving crew? Were you in the Far East blowing up the Chinese while the rest of us were in high school?"

Andrei jerked his head towards me and retorted, "Our Nastia was blowing up White Guardsmen before she ate solid food." Everybody laughed.

That was, indirectly, a true statement. None of my friends had ever made it past my father without hearing the story of how I started out life as a loyal Communist baby.

"Well, she doesn't *look* like a soldier," the physics student replied, sulking.

I felt suddenly self-conscious about my flowered summer dress and my sandals. My hair was pinned up in a braid around my head like a wreath – just like any girl on any Sunday afternoon in June. I told the student, "We're flight instructors. I'm a pilot. Like Marina Raskova."

Marina Raskova was everyone's hero – even if you weren't a pilot yourself. We'd all had our ears glued to the radio three years ago as Marina Raskova had smashed to smithereens the women's record for a long-distance flight as she crossed the Soviet Union. She'd been navigating for two other female pilots, and when their plane had unexpectedly run out of fuel, Marina Raskova had parachuted out over the Siberian wilderness. She'd had to spend ten days living on berries and fighting off bears before she was rescued. For a year afterwards, I'd carried her photograph in my schoolbag to inspire me.

"Oh!" the physics student said, and his face lit up with recognition. "A pilot like Marina Raskova, of course. I should have known – you have the same hair-do."

I couldn't tell if he was mocking me or if he was serious. Marina Raskova was the greatest woman pilot-navigator of our time – a wilderness survivor, a career military officer and a mother – and all this student could remember was her hair-do!

But before I could defend Marina Raskova – and all women pilots in general – the door to the office opened. A young man came out and strode away down the passage, and another young man in uniform stuck his head out the door and called Stefan's name.

Stefan glanced at me and grinned. I knew he was telling me to forget about the humourless university student. Now was our chance.

"Come on," Stefan said, and he waved one arm to usher us ahead of him.

There were protests both in the passage and in the office as we all trooped in together. But the nine of us were so united that it was easier for the man in uniform to let us line up inside the office than to try to shoo us away.

The office was dark, with blinds drawn against the glaring midsummer sunlight. The window was propped open and a small electric fan whined on the desk next to a telephone. Behind the desk, the overworked Komsomol recruitment officer wiped his red and sweating face. He frowned hard at us.

"Stefan?" the officer rumbled. "I only called in Stefan Dmitrievich."

Big Stefan stepped forward with his normal calm confidence. "I'm here with my companions," he said.

Before the officer could breathe another word, Stefan explained that we were a team of qualified pilots and flight instructors. "We want to serve together," Stefan finished firmly.

The Komsomol officer raised his hand in a gesture meant to command silence. Then, with a big sigh, he picked up the telephone. He didn't look at any of us as he asked for a connection to an air force academy we'd never heard of. After a moment, he began to speak.

"I have eight pilots for you," the officer told the person at the other end of the line.

Stefan opened his mouth to interrupt, and again the officer's hand sprang up, warning Stefan to be quiet.

"Yes," the red-faced officer said into the telephone. "They are all flight instructors. Each one has more than five hundred hours' flight time. Yes – all of them are ready to leave today."

He listened impatiently as sweat streamed down his face.

"Very good," the officer said at last. "Thank you."

He hung up and made a note on one of his forms.

Big Stefan took a step forward and drew a deep breath. Without asking permission to speak, he said, "Nine, sir."

The Komsomol officer looked up, his face perplexed. "Nine what?" he asked.

"You told the air force academy you had eight pilots for them," Big Stefan replied. "But there are nine of us."

"Oh!" The officer glanced at me for a moment. I met his gaze. "The girl too?" he asked. "Just a moment …"

He picked up the telephone again. I thought he was going to make another call to the academy. He had to wait for a line, so we all had to wait along with him.

"Give me the Leningrad Youth Aeroclub," the officer said at last.

After another moment, the officer said, "Hello! I'd like to speak to the Chief Flight Instructor, please."

He hadn't called the air force academy this time. He'd called our boss.

CHAPTER 4

The Chief Flight Instructor was the only other woman besides me who taught at the Leningrad Youth Aeroclub.

We were all a bit scared of the Chief. She was an abrasive, loud woman with bleached blonde hair, a tightly belted waist and a face that was always heavy with powder and lipstick. But she was a good teacher and a superb pilot, and she stood up for us. I wouldn't have been accepted into the aeroclub three years before if she hadn't convinced the medical officer that I wasn't finished growing (I was).

The Chief had known my parents for a long time. They'd met during the Civil War, but none of them would tell me how. Once or twice a year, the Chief would come over and drink vodka with my parents, and I would have to go and spend the night with my granny so that I wouldn't be shocked by their talk of their memories of war.

It was the Chief who convinced my father to let me learn to fly. Men and women might be equal according to the Stalin Constitution, but my father was uncomfortable with me doing what he considered to be a man's job. And he worried that flight training was too dangerous for an after-school activity. When I told the Chief about this, she came striding into my family's apartment. There she explained, loudly, that if she didn't train me to be a first-rate pilot, my father could come and shoot her in the heart.

"You know I would never do that," my father told the Chief mildly. "Not after what you've been through." She'd had a hard time in the Civil War. She'd even lost three of her lower teeth in some past battle.

Now the impatient, red-faced Komsomol officer was talking to the Chief over the telephone. I hoped she'd tell him the same thing she told my father three years ago.

"I've got a handful of your pilots here," the officer said to the Chief. "They want to fly to war and shoot down German fascists. Any objections?"

Whatever the Chief's response was, it made the Komsomol officer laugh. "Yes, the girl is here too.

But I have to make sure you're not short of staff,"
the officer said. "We can't risk all our glorious
nation's flight instructors ending up ..."

He bit his lip and turned redder.

We all guessed the officer had been going to
say he couldn't risk us all ending up dead.

Andrei and Ivan swapped nervous glances. The
Komsomol officer tried to think of a better word
and then laughed again.

"You'll be short of staff if they all end up
promoted!" the officer finished in triumph.

After finishing the conversation, the Komsomol
officer hung up for the second time and scribbled
another note. Then he read off a list of names.

All the boys were on it. But I was not.

"Go to the mustering point in Uritsky Square,"
the officer instructed. "You'll be assigned to
a regiment and given uniforms. You'll travel
together to Bataisk, to the school for fighter pilots."

Did he mean all of us? He still hadn't read my
name.

"Go on, what are you waiting for?" the officer said, now with irritation in his voice as well as impatience.

"Sir," Andrei said. "What about Nastia?"

The Komsomol officer wiped his sweating forehead again and looked down at his notes.

"Ah, yes, the girl. Nastia Nabokova, you are to report back to your Chief Flight Instructor at the Leningrad Youth Aeroclub to resume your flight instructor duties."

"*What?*" I said.

All eight of my friends exploded with outrage on my account.

"But Nastia's been flying *longer* than the rest of us!" Andrei said.

"She started when she was in ninth grade in high school," Val explained. "The Chief let her in underage because she'd studied flight theory outside school hours."

"Nastia worked as a mechanic for a year too!" Andrei added. "And her father and mother ..."

Everybody gave me apologetic glances. My friends knew it embarrassed me when people talked about my parents and their heroic past.

Big Stefan said, "Nastia's parents were Communist Party members when it *started*."

That sounded almost like a threat. I thought I saw a shadow of doubt drift over the Komsomol officer's face.

"Stop boasting about my parents," I said to Stefan and turned to the Komsomol officer myself. "Sir! I want to go and fight the German fascists with my companions. Why are you sending me back to the aeroclub?"

"You will take your orders from your Chief Flight Instructor," the officer insisted. "There is important war work for you here in Leningrad." He leaned forward, his forehead shining with sweat. "Go on! You have all been given assignments. I do not have time to waste arguing with young people! Go!"

CHAPTER 5

None of my friends said anything until we'd left the building.

Then Stefan spoke. "Just come with us anyway. No one will ever know you weren't sent on purpose. They'll just think it was an office error. You saw how messed-up that guy's desk was."

I sighed.

"No, I'd better not," I said. "If I don't report to the Chief, it's bound to get her in trouble."

You see what a good young Komsomol member I was? I did as I was told.

My friends all hugged me goodbye. There were tears in Big Stefan's eyes and in Ivan's.

But nobody cried. As I turned to go, Stefan saluted me. I saluted back.

I wondered if I'd ever see any of them again. I knew they were wondering the same thing.

But we went.

★

When I got to the aeroclub, the Chief was sitting on the lower wing of one of our utility training aircraft. The "Corn-duster", it was called – a small biplane that was the heart and soul of every Soviet flight school. I'd completed my first solo flight in a plane like this when I was sixteen. I could pull it out of a spin with my eyes closed. It wasn't an air force fighter plane, but I could fly it as well as any pilot in Leningrad.

The Chief looked so relaxed as she tried to stay cool in the shade of the Corn-duster's upper wing. She was slowly smoking a cigarette and gazing at the sky, as if she wondered when the weather was going to change.

As I walked towards her, the Chief's calm pose made me aware that my own fists were clenched shut. I made myself open my hands, thinking about it as I'd done three years ago, when the Chief was teaching me to fly: "Lightly, lightly!" she would say, in her weird accent – as if she was imitating the King of England speaking Russian. The Chief's missing teeth gave her a slight lisp. "Hold the control stick as if it were an egg. A Fabergé Easter egg – a jewelled golden shell. It's a control stick, not a pistol you're going to fire! You're not shooting the Czar. You're flying a plane. Pretend it will break if you squeeze too hard. Lightly, and you'll feel the plane responding!"

I stood next to the Corn-duster, in the shadow of its upper wing. Without a word, the Chief held out her cigarette. I didn't smoke then, but I took the cigarette anyway. I knew the Chief meant it as a small gift to console me.

When she still didn't say anything, I burst out in frustration, "The Komsomol officer said you were going to give me an assignment!"

"You're the last instructor I have left," the Chief told me.

It wasn't much of an answer, but I knew from experience I wouldn't get anywhere if I got angry or questioned the Chief. I waited, gripping the burning cigarette she'd given me, and wondered what she was thinking. I knew she'd only tell me what she wanted me to know, and only when she was ready.

★

The Chief was older than the other flight instructors. How much older was a mystery. She claimed not to know the year she'd been born. "I think it was the year before the war," she'd say if you asked. But it was never clear if she meant the Great War in Europe, which would have made her twenty-eight, or the war with Japan, which would have made her thirty-eight. She couldn't have meant the Civil War, because that's when she met my parents. I knew the Chief must be nearly as old as they were, even if she seemed younger.

She didn't have any family at all – no parents, no brothers or sisters, no husband, no children, nor a sweetheart that any of us knew about. She didn't even have a dog. She worked and ate and slept at the aeroclub, and she was addicted to films and taking photographs of planes.

She was not an ideal of Soviet womanhood.

Despite her belted waist and made-up face, she was no beauty. She had battle scars – a long silver ridge that split her hairline, from a wound that had healed without being stitched. There was another like it under her jaw. When the weather was warm and the Chief wore short sleeves, you could see that the skin of her arms was peppered with more scars, as if riddled with termites.

But you couldn't see the three missing teeth in her lower jaw unless she smiled very broadly. She was short and stout and plain-faced under the make-up, and she dressed like a man even when she wasn't at the aeroclub. When she flew, she wore a tightly belted flight suit over her blouse and trousers.

Yet there was rumour, among some of the older male instructors – not *my* friends! – that the Chief wore extremely lacy French underwear.

The Chief was a good instructor, but she was not sympathetic. She couldn't tolerate stupidity. She didn't even tolerate students who couldn't understand her weird lisping accent.

But while the Chief talked loudly and laughed loudly, she worked tirelessly to train young Soviet pilots. You could not fault her for that.

And in the air, her flight was as fearless and natural as that of a bird.

She ruled the airfield like an empress.

★

"What do you mean, I'm your last instructor?" I asked the Chief as I held the cigarette.

"All our instructors have joined the air force except you," the Chief said. "You have to stay here to train new pilots."

"But—" I began, but I couldn't get past the first word of my sentence. I took a drag on the cigarette the Chief had given me, even though I didn't smoke, and after I finished coughing I tried again.

"But—"

Again I choked and gagged on the smoke. The Chief rolled her eyes and held out her hand. I gave her back the cigarette.

"*But* you tried to enlist," the Chief filled in for me. "Yes, I know. I told them you were just as good a pilot as the boys. Better, even. But they sent you back here anyway, because you're a girl. Of course. They don't like sending girls to be killed."

She gave a sarcastic snort and continued, "They don't like sending girls to be killed, and they're going to have a shortage of instructors to train new boys – to replace all those who are about to get killed by the German fascists. But don't worry. You won't miss anything yet. We don't have any aircraft apart from these Corn-duster trainers, and we won't be going to war in *them*."

"I would go—"

The Chief cut me off. "I don't mean we don't have any other aircraft here at this aeroclub. I mean *nowhere in Russia* do we have any aircraft. The Luftwaffe bombers of the German air force destroyed all of our aircraft this morning."

I stared at her.

The Chief shrugged. She stubbed out her cigarette on the sole of her boot.

"Surprise attack," she explained. "They bombed all our airfields at dawn. They destroyed our air force *on the ground*. Now their troops are pushing across our borders in a battle front that stretches from the Baltic Sea to the Black Sea. They're eating up our nation as they burn and kill their way across our land, aiming for our big cities, Leningrad and Moscow."

She let that sink in.

Then she said, "Our glorious leader, Stalin, is keeping very quiet, so that's what the rest of us have to do too."

"I don't want to keep quiet!" I cried. "I want to fight! I want to chase the fascist army out! What can I do? All I can do is fly! I want to use that! I want to help!"

The Chief shrugged again and told me, "You can do what I'm doing. Write to Marina Raskova. She's got the ear of our glorious leader. Stalin listens to her – who knows why. If anyone can make an argument for letting women fly in this air war, it'll be Marina Raskova. And in the meantime ..." The Chief paused to flick the dead butt of her cigarette into the grass. "In the meantime, you and I have to train new pilots. So that when our glorious factories produce some glorious new airplanes, there will be someone to fly them."

I wondered what would happen to my friends. I wondered where they would be sent and how long it would be before they were armed and fighting – protecting the blue skies of our Motherland from the enemy invaders.

The Chief added, "When you've trained fifty new pilots, I'll have another word with the Komsomol officer about sending you somewhere you can fight."

I knew it was true that we'd need new pilots, and I knew that I could train them.

"I'll do it," I said slowly, "if you promise to keep your word."

"When have I not?" the Chief said. "Of course I'll keep my word."

PART 2: LATE SUMMER, 1941

Leningrad, in the air

CHAPTER 6

I kept a tally of my new pilots, counting them up as the invading German fascists swept closer and closer to Leningrad.

The Germans ate up more and more of our Motherland with every step they took. They burned homes and seized our crops and left their soldiers in every broken village to establish German rules there. Our own Red Army could not stop them. Every day that summer, every time I went flying with a student, we would take off over the defences that were being erected around Leningrad to protect the city. Every day, I could see from the air that the battle front was moving nearer to Leningrad by the minute.

I wasn't going to be able to train anywhere near fifty students before the Germans got here.

Then one sunny morning early in September, the Chief sent all but eight of the students home. To the remaining eight, who were confident enough to fly solo, and to me, she made an announcement.

She gathered us on the airfield, her sleeves rolled up so her scars showed.

"We have twenty-four hours to evacuate the airfield," she said, her voice matter-of-fact. "Each of you is going to have to fly one of the aeroclub planes away from Leningrad. You can have the rest of the morning off while the mechanics fuel up and check the aircraft. Be back here at noon, ready for a two o'clock take-off. We fly to Moscow."

We were silent.

To explain, the Chief added, "The German fascists will be here, attacking the city, in less than a week. We need to save our training aircraft from them."

One of the mechanics was waving to the Chief from over by the hangars, looking as if he had a question. The Chief started walking towards him, then stopped and turned back to the rest of us. She warned, "Make sure you bring a winter coat with you. It might be a while before we get back."

★

I went home to my parents' flat to get my winter coat. The electricity in their building wasn't connected for some reason – we'd been warned to conserve power, so maybe the caretaker had already switched it off, even before the city was attacked. The lift was out of order, so I had to climb five flights of stairs to the flat. No one was there, of course – my father was at work and my mother was digging trenches around the city, as she'd been doing all summer.

I had the envelope with my last month's pay in my pocket. I took it out and wrote with a china pencil, the kind you use for planning your flight route on a map:

Dear Mum and Dad, I am helping to evacuate the aeroclub planes to Moscow. I don't know when we're coming back.

It seemed too short, so I added:

I will write and write and write to you, and when I can't write, I will be thinking of you and of Leningrad.

That seemed sentimental.

I'm off to begin a new life!

I signed it, "Your loving daughter, Nastia."

I left the envelope on my mother's work table and locked up the apartment once more. I still had most of the morning left.

The Alexander Palace, where my father worked, was in a park about twenty-five kilometres south of the city. I'd often flown over it in peacetime, dipping my wings from side to side in case my father was looking. I knew he'd wave up at me even if I couldn't see him.

If I went back to the aeroclub now, I'd have time to fly over my city and wave my wings at my father from the sky.

★

I had to tell some of the ground crew about my plan, because they were getting the planes ready for the evacuation. I couldn't just take one without explaining what I was doing. But I didn't say anything to the Chief, because I didn't want to give her the chance to say no to me.

The mechanics never said no to me. They weren't happy about it that day, but they let me take a plane anyway. A couple of them helped me to wheel one of the Corn-dusters onto the airfield.

After I'd climbed into the cockpit, one of the mechanics swung the propeller to get the engine started for me. My heart leaped into life with the engine. I was excited about my sentimental farewell tour as I took off over Leningrad.

To the north, I could see the Neva River winding through the city, and the Gulf of Finland shining dark blue beyond it. There were big barrage balloons floating in the air around the outside of Leningrad, tethered to the ground with steel cables. I knew they'd be loaded with explosives to try to snarl up enemy aircraft. I flew carefully around them.

I could see the ditches that everyone in the city was helping to dig to protect Leningrad from the invading German army. These trenches were already filled with guns and bales of barbed wire to try to stop the fascists sweeping into the city. I flew low, looking out of my open cockpit and waving. Tiny figures looked up from their work and waved back.

Maybe my mother could see me. Somewhere down there, she was helping to dig those ditches. I pictured her hair tied up in a blue scarf, blisters forming on her soft hands – hands that had only handled a typewriter for the past fifteen years.

But she'd been a soldier before – she wouldn't complain.

I thought of my mother sneaking her messages past guards, with me, her screaming baby, in her arms. I thought of bullets glancing off diamonds hidden in stiff lace underwear, and my father driving that truck heavy with the bodies of murdered girls my own age. I thought of the Chief getting her teeth knocked out in close combat long ago. I thought of my father packing up antique amber and silver dishes in a hurry so that they could be hidden from the enemy invaders.

I turned south to fly to the Alexander Palace.

CHAPTER 7

As I flew, I could see a line of smoke staining the blue sky on my right side. That was the Front – the line made by the invading army of German fascists as they mowed and burned their way across my homeland. They'd created a bloody battleground that stretched over fifteen hundred kilometres from north to south.

Today, the Front was very near. Today, with my thoughts full of the Chief's teeth and my mother's screaming baby and Anastasia Romanova's diamond-studded underwear, the war became real to me for the first time. I could *see* it, and it was getting *close*. In another two or three days, the enemy army would be there, below me.

I'd reached the Alexander Palace now, in the sprawl of palaces and parkland on the edge of the town of Pushkin. Below, the elegant buildings looked like puzzles lying in a bed of soft green velvet. I tried to picture how this scene would change in a few weeks' time, when the Germans got here. There would be soldiers darting and shooting from behind the white trunks of the birch trees beneath me. Tanks would lumber up the long drive and park in front of the palace.

It wasn't hard to imagine. There was a lot of activity already. Trucks were travelling to and fro as they carried the museum's treasures to a safer place, and I could see workers digging around the fountains in the park.

I hadn't thought that the Germans might have sent some of their *Luftwaffe* aircraft to check out the Alexander Palace grounds ahead of time.

I was still heading south. When I looked to my right, above the oily cloud of the Front, a black speck danced before my eyes, growing steadily larger.

At first I thought it was a bird – a crow or, no, an eagle – as it sped towards me in a dive from above. I was startled but not afraid. I lowered the nose of my plane so I could get out of the way.

Then the sky around me seemed to explode.

The black spot before my eyes had become a German fighter plane – a Messerschmitt Me-109, to be precise. The German pilot had taken me completely by surprise. He'd come at me with the

sun at his back. And I was so new to war that I had
not even been looking for him.

I could hear his machine-gun fire rattling
like drums over the chattering engine of my
Corn-duster. When the fighter swooped down over
my open cockpit, the roar of his powerful engine
was so deafening that it even drowned out his
gunfire. I wanted to wrap my arms over my head,
but that would have meant letting go of the control
stick.

And I was not going to do that.

My plane had no guns, and the Messerschmitt
was four times as fast. I could not fight back, and I
could not outrace the German fighter. But maybe,
if I did not lose my nerve, I could outfly him.

I pushed the control stick further forward and
shoved on full power so that my plane was now
screaming towards the ground at high speed. I
didn't dare look up to check, but I hoped that the
Messerschmitt had swooped away after his first
plunge at me. I knew he'd circle back after me –
but maybe, if I got low enough, he'd lose sight of
my fabric wings against the landscape below. He
might miss me among the fountains and hedges
and statues in the leafy parks around the palace.

Another burst of machine-gun fire tore into my wings. I pushed my plane into a steeper dive. The increased gravity made me dizzy. As the ground came rushing to meet me, I managed to level the wings of my Corn-duster to fly just above the rooftops of the Alexander Palace. I was heading for a strip of meadow at the edge of the birch trees in the woodland on its west side.

Black figures rushed below me like ants, pointing up at the sky. I saw small puffs of smoke around them. The people working in the grounds of the Alexander Palace were firing guns at the Messerschmitt.

I could hear the plane screaming after me, then away from me and back again. The Messerschmitt was so much faster than my Corn-duster that it kept overtaking me. The pilot couldn't make his powerful plane fly *slowly* enough to keep his guns aimed at me. He kept having to circle back to get in another shot.

The white birch trees in the park rose ahead of me. I wanted to land right in front of them. I muttered to myself the old rowing countdown:

"*In – three. In – two. In – one!*"

I cut the power. The wheels of the Leningrad Youth Aeroclub Corn-duster touched down lightly on the edge of the park.

I scrambled out of the cockpit even before my plane had rolled to a stop. I covered my head with my arms and sprinted for the safety of the trees.

The Messerschmitt came roaring back, its machine-gun fire louder than anything I'd ever heard. It was like laying your head on a railway track as a train approached.

As I hid from the sky among the birch trees, I turned to watch. The German fighter filled the wings and body of my plane with bullet holes.

And then he roared away.

CHAPTER 8

I waited, frozen in my hiding place between the birch trees. Would he come back? In the distance I could hear the boom of big guns – I guessed it was our soldiers in the town of Pushkin opening fire on the German plane. And while my heart was still thundering, I realised that the Messerschmitt pilot wasn't invincible, even with his sleek, superior aircraft and his powerful cannons. He wouldn't want to be shot down in flames or captured by the enemy for the sake of one unarmed Corn-duster.

He didn't come back.

Even so, I stayed huddled among the wild flowers at the foot of the birch trees for a few more minutes, with my arms still over my head.

It was the first time anyone had fired a gun at me intending to kill me, and I was ashamed of myself for being so frightened.

For a brief moment, I wondered what those young daughters of Czar Nicholas II must have felt in the seconds when they knew they were going to die in a storm of gunfire. I also wondered, very babyishly indeed, if their ghosts haunted this parkland where they used to play, and if they were laughing at me.

★

When I'd recovered enough to get to my feet, I began to pick my way through the meadow to get back to my plane and look at the damage.

There were so many holes in the fabric wings that I couldn't count them. There were at least thirty in the body of the plane itself. I realised how lucky I was that there weren't any holes in *me*.

"Oh, what will Dad say?" I burst out, feeling so miserable I spoke aloud. And then, "*What will the Chief say?*"

The propeller seemed all right. In fact, apart from the bullet holes, my plane still seemed to be in one piece. I'd landed it smoothly, and the undercarriage was fine. There wasn't any mechanical reason I shouldn't be able to take off again from this meadow in the Alexander Park and fly back to the aeroclub in time for the evacuation.

But I wasn't looking forward to facing the Chief.

I gritted my teeth. I didn't have a choice. I hunted around to find a pair of stout stones I could use to chock the wheels. I needed to keep the plane from moving while I swung the propeller to start the engine.

Then I heard a voice shouting my name.

"Nastia? *Nastia!*"

And there was my father himself, leading a search party from the Alexander Palace.

I was twice lucky today, I realised. I'd been shot down by an enemy fighter plane for the first time, but I wasn't hurt. And now my own father was right here to make sure I was still alive.

I was too shaken to run to him, but he ran towards me.

"*Nastia!*" my father called.

I shuddered. A small crowd of men was with my father, their eyes concerned and curious. I couldn't break down and cry in front of them. I had to pretend I was fine.

"Hi, Dad," I said, clenching my fists so he wouldn't see them shaking. And then I unclenched them very carefully, just the way I'd done the day the war started.

Dad scooped me into his arms in a bear hug.

"I thought it might be you!" he cried. "What was that fascist bastard doing, attacking an unarmed flying school plane? We tried to get him—"

He hugged me again. His comrades were exclaiming in loud voices, congratulating me on my escape.

"I need to get back to the aeroclub," I said. "We're evacuating our planes to Moscow this afternoon. I don't know how long we'll be gone – the Chief told us to bring winter coats."

"Oh no," my father said. "I'm not going to let you rush off right away after a scare like this. Haste makes people stupid. Believe me, I know. And if you're setting out on a long voyage, you're supposed to pretend you're not going anywhere in a hurry. Come, walk around the park with me before you go to war."

So I did.

We walked past the Alexander Palace and looked at the fountains in the Catherine Park. My father showed me what he was working on – they were burying the famous bronze statue of the girl with the pitcher so that the fascists couldn't find it.

"Rub her foot for good luck," my father said. "She's been here in the park for over two hundred years, with water flowing from her broken pitcher. You could both use some luck."

So I rubbed the cool metal. The bronze girl's toes shone brassy gold at the end of her brown foot, the result of generations of girls just like me caressing them for luck.

"She was here a hundred years before the Revolution, and she's still here," my father said. "When this war is over, she'll still be here. And we'll dust her off and she'll have a new life in a new garden."

Then we walked back to my tattered Corn-duster and kissed each other goodbye.

"The Chief will take good care of you," Dad told me. "She is a fighter and a survivor."

"I know," I said, and I thought of those missing teeth again.

"She and I were comrades in the Revolution, before I met your mother," my father said. "The

Chief's father was a military man, a colonel who was disgraced in the Great War. The Chief had to make a new life for herself, beyond his shadow. She'll show you how to do it. Stay close to her, Nastia."

"I'll be fine," I said. "Isn't that what my name means? Rebirth."

"Yes." My father smiled. "And she chose that name for you. The Chief will take care of you, believe me."

"I do believe you," I said.

My father hugged me again. "Write to us!" he said.

"I will! Give Mum a kiss from me!"

"I will."

I felt oddly calm after this false half an hour of peace. I climbed into the cockpit of the Corn-duster, with both me and the plane a bit more experienced in the art of war than we had been that morning.

As I took off again, my back crawled with the fear that the Messerschmitt fighter, or another like it, would come screaming out of the sky behind me. Its cannons would thunder, and this time the bullets wouldn't miss me. But the sky was empty on the way back to the aeroclub.

I flew over the length of Nevsky Prospekt, Leningrad's beautiful main street. I could see that it was packed with automobiles and horses and baby carriages and bicycles. Some people were trying to leave the city or sending their children away, while others would be hurrying to stock up on food and torches and candles. Below me, tiny figures on ladders were boarding up shop windows. Everyone was getting ready for the city to be attacked.

I wondered if my friends from the rowing club had come under fire yet. I wondered if they were already flying in armed combat against an enemy like the one I'd met an hour ago.

I wondered if they were still alive. It was over two months since I'd seen them. I thought of Big Stefan, always so calm and deliberate. Surely he was still alive.

I might never find out. I didn't even know where to write to him.

CHAPTER 9

"Where the hell have you been, Nastia Nabokova?" the Chief barked at me as I climbed out of the battered Corn-duster. "This is no time to be sightseeing at the aeroclub's expense! We're evacuating today, and I told you to be back here at noon."

As she came closer to the plane and saw the tattered wings, her thin painted eyebrows flew into tiny arches of surprise. "What the hell happened?" she demanded.

"I met a fascist fighter," I said.

The Chief went up to the plane and ran her hands over the holes in the lower wing. Then she turned back to me and said, "You were lucky."

"I know," I agreed.

Her face and voice were filled with cold fury. "You don't have *any idea*."

The Chief pulled at the shredded fabric around one of the holes and tore a strip out of the wing. Then she tore at another.

"See this? What if your fascist fighter had been using tracer? You know what that is? Incendiary bullets? No, you don't know. Bullets that are on fire. They light up so a pilot can see where he's shooting. If your fascist fighter had hit you with just one tracer bullet, this plane would have burned up like a torch – like a firework. *Whoof!* One bullet, and you'd have been a shooting star, my Nastia."

The Chief gave a bark of mirthless laughter and added, "Or a normal bullet could have hit the engine. Or the fuel tanks. And then also, *Whoof!* Fireworks."

She waved a dismissive hand at the plane. "You were luckier than you know," she said, then she scowled. "There isn't time to replace the entire skin of the aircraft, but see if you can get the mechanics to tape it up. If you can't, you'll have to fly with it full of holes. Why the hell did you take a plane up *today*?"

"I wanted to wave goodbye to my father," I explained.

It sounded childish. The Chief was not sympathetic, but she was curious.

"Did you see him?" she asked.

"Yes. I landed there after I was attacked. That's why I took so long – I walked around the Catherine Park with him. And I got to say goodbye to the girl with the broken pitcher."

This amused the Chief. She gave her wolfhound bark of a laugh and asked, "Did you rub her toes for luck? Of course you did. That old superstition! Don't you think the Czar's dead children did the same thing before *they* left the Alexander Palace for their long journey to Siberia? And look what happened to them."

For so many reasons, I wished she would just *shut up* about the Czar's dead children.

But I didn't dare say that to her.

"Come on," the Chief told me. "You'll have to refuel even if we can't do anything about the bullet holes. I want every aircraft full, and you've used an hour's worth of fuel at least. Anything still in the storage tanks will have to stay here, and anything that stays here has to be destroyed." She spat on the ground beneath the plane. "We don't

want the German fascists getting their hands on
our leftover fuel."

★

It was terrible to fly away from the Leningrad
Youth Aeroclub, leaving the city behind to be
attacked.

It was the second time that day I had fled from
the fascists. I hated having to run away – to fly
away – from my city. But what could I do? I had no
weapons. I had no armour. I could not fight back.
This was the only way I could help.

I took off in my bandaged plane. I carried one
of the mechanics in the cockpit behind me – he'd
just finished setting fire to the fuel depot. As our
Corn-duster lifted off from the airfield, the club's
fuel tanks exploded in a blast of red and orange
flames. Black smoke billowed below us. Across the
airfield, the hangars and clubhouse were already
burning.

As I took off, I could also see the line of fire
and smoke ahead of me that was the Front – and
it seemed nearer now than it had been when I'd
taken off earlier that morning.

I thought of my father, wrapping up the dead Romanov family's crystal glasses in cotton wool. I thought of my mother coming home to an apartment without electricity to find my scribbled farewell note lying on the table.

I imagined German soldiers swarming down Nevsky Prospekt with their guns blazing, firing into the crowds on the streets.

My parents didn't have diamonds sewn into their underwear. And it wouldn't have helped them if they had.

PART 3: AUTUMN, 1941

Moscow

CHAPTER 10

Two days later, we refugees from Leningrad arrived with our small flock of Corn-dusters at the Russian Air Force Academy outside Moscow. I'd never seen an airfield so busy. Half a dozen flying clubs had evacuated their planes to the same place. Right away, the Chief and I got separated from our students as the airfield authorities split the men and women into different groups. Suddenly I was among more female flyers than I'd known existed. All of them, like me, had tried to volunteer for the air force – and they'd all been told, like me, that they had to stay behind and train young men to fly.

For our quarters, the women were given a section of the local pilots' canteen full of folding wooden army camp beds. It was a warm September night, and the Chief dragged her camp bed outside. I hesitated to leave the rest of the group, but my father had told me to stay close to the Chief, so I set up my bed there too.

"As good as your bunk at the aeroclub back in Leningrad?" the Chief teased me.

"Better," I said. "I slept on an army camp bed all my life. My father said it would make me strong and adaptable. Czar Nicholas II's daughters all slept on camp beds too, my dad said, even when they lived in the Alexander Palace. It was so they wouldn't grow up soft. Dad said that what was good enough for them was good enough for me."

"Ha!" the Chief laughed. "The only thing your father ever got wrong was trying to keep you on the ground." She lay on her back gazing up at the sky, and when she spoke again her tone was blissful. "I also slept on an army camp bed all my life. Look at those stars!"

And they really were beautiful. I wouldn't have noticed if I hadn't gone out there after her.

★

The day after we got to Moscow, the German forces began their bombardment of Leningrad.

We all had our ears glued to the radio, waiting to hear if the city had fallen. But it hadn't.

70

"Leningrad remains strong," the radio announcer said. "Today, the fascist army has blockaded our beautiful historic city. Bombs and guns encircle the city on every side, but we will not let them in. The citizens of Leningrad are prepared – we will fight back."

It was impossible not to think of my mother and father under attack – of the guns battering at the city just as they'd battered my plane for five minutes in the air. My parents might be prepared, but there was no relief or escape for them.

"We'll fight back till we run out of ammunition," one of the other young women beside me whispered. "If we're surrounded …"

She didn't finish her sentence. No one here knew each other well enough to risk saying anything negative about the way the war was going – yet it was clearly already a disaster. We were all nervous and feared someone reporting us to the Komsomol …

"Now Moscow must fortify herself against the fascist invaders too," the urgent voice from the radio continued. "The German army is sweeping across Russia and all the Soviet states in a battle front nearly two thousand kilometres long. The invaders have rolled across our fertile fields in the Ukraine, destroying our crops and burning villages. Our people must fight back. Moscow must fight back! Citizens, you must leave your homes and prepare for war! Young men, to your tanks, take up your rifles! Students, take up spades and dig trenches for our defensive guns! Your local Party committee will tell you how you can help."

The whole roomful of women sighed. Yes, some of us were students and could help to dig trenches. But no one had mentioned how women could help to *fight*.

And then, as if he'd heard us, the radio presenter continued:

"And now, young women of our glorious nation, we have a message especially for you – from our celebrated aviator, hero of the Soviet Union, Major Marina Raskova."

"Oh!" we cried together.

Around the room, we frustrated young pilots leaned forward to listen to our hero. The familiar voice of our beloved Major Raskova, warm and encouraging, came over the radio. We listened, spellbound, and her words gave us hope.

"Dear sisters! All you millions of Soviet women who work tirelessly every day in our fields and factories, who give your strength and spirit to the Motherland! Come together now, all you mothers and daughters, labourers, scientists, doctors, tractor-drivers and pilots! The time has come to strike back against the bloody aggression of fascism! Women of our Motherland, stand together now as freedom fighters!"

Afterwards, we all had to go and dig trenches. There wasn't anything else for us to do yet, and there wasn't extra fuel for the planes we'd brought with us. But now we had hope that after we'd fortified the capital city we might be able to help with the fight.

CHAPTER 11

We dug trenches for exactly one month. On the first hot and dusty day of digging, when I stood still for a moment to stretch my back, I noticed that some high-school girls from Moscow had all stripped down to their underwear. One of them saw me looking at them and blushed.

"We volunteered on the day of the invasion," the blushing girl explained. "You know, that Sunday in June? We came out here in the dresses we were wearing, and we've been digging in our underwear all summer to save them!"

I was better off than they were – when I left Leningrad I'd taken along a change of clothes and a sweater as well as that winter coat the Chief had warned us to bring. Also, my log book with my flight records, and my Komsomol card, of course. But the clothes might have to last me the whole winter. I gave the Chief a questioning glance, and she read my mind.

"Oh, go on," the Chief said, giving me permission to copy the girls.

It was a lot more comfortable digging in fewer clothes.

The Chief didn't join us. She kept herself buttoned up to the neck, even when her blouse was damp with sweat and sticking to her back.

I bet she'd rather ruin her clothes than show her fancy underwear, I thought.

The Chief had brought along even fewer personal items than me. But among these were a few things I considered completely inessential. In addition to three bottles of peroxide, she had a beautiful varnished box painted with a picture of a firebird with an eagle's wings and a woman's face. In the box were five different shades of lipstick, a pair of tweezers, a small tin of rouge and a kohl pencil for drawing her fake eyebrows. Plus a compact mirror and face powder. She was careful only to apply small amounts of this magical collection to her face each day, not knowing when she'd ever get her hands on more.

Even on that first morning of digging trenches, the Chief painted her lips with a thin layer of bright pink. Anything else would have streaked and smeared when she began to sweat, so she didn't waste it.

It's like armour, I thought. *She uses it like armour. When her face is painted, she's not just behind a mask – she's behind a helmet. It makes her strong.*

I wished I felt as confident about anything. I had no armour. I felt lost. What was I doing in Moscow digging ditches? The only life I knew was in Leningrad, and in the air.

★

As we hurried to build last-minute fortifications around the capital city, the German army moved steadily, terribly, relentlessly closer.

By the beginning of October, everyone knew the invaders were now only days away from Moscow.

Back home, the city of Leningrad was under attack. The Germans hadn't managed to get past our defences there, but nobody else could get in or out. Everything in Leningrad was running short – food, fuel, medicine, weapons. And every day the German guns and bombs thundered into the city from across the blockade.

Seeing what was happening to Leningrad, now Moscow too was emptying. People were leaving the city in trainloads. Whole factories, with all their workers and production lines, were being shipped to the far corners of the Soviet Union. Theatre and ballet companies were leaving. Works of art were packed up and stowed on trains and in trucks. The preserved body of our glorious revolutionary leader, Vladimir Lenin, was disturbed from his sleep in the mausoleum in Red Square and packed up to move to Siberia. There, he could continue to inspire generations of Soviet children – if there were any left when all this was over.

A squadron of air force pilots in trucks turned up one day and flew all our aeroclub Corn-dusters away so someone else could use them to drop small bombs on the German battle lines.

I – and the other young women pilots – felt we could have easily performed that task ourselves if they'd let us. But we weren't allowed a moment's outrage.

"We're moving!" the Chief announced, and there was excitement and hope in her harsh, lisping voice. "Get your things, girls! Marina Raskova has *done it*."

"Done what? What's going on?" we asked.

"Marina Raskova has permission from our glorious leader to put together a unit of women pilots. She's going to oversee our training. She has permission from *Stalin himself*. We report today!"

I'd never felt sure that the Chief's enthusiasm for our glorious leader was real. But the emotion in her announcement about Marina Raskova was real enough.

"*Today?*" we all gasped.

"Today," the Chief replied.

Months of frustration, months of exhaustion, months of fear – these all faded in an instant.

"We're going to be evacuated again," the Chief explained. "But we'll go as part of an aviation unit, not to dig more ditches as refugees. Pack your things."

That was our final day as young women in limbo – digging ditches and staring at the sky, worrying that we'd be killed by falling bombs and working in our underwear to save our clothes.

The next day we were soldiers.

CHAPTER 12

As new recruits of the Soviet armed forces, we were given men's uniforms. Nothing fit anybody, and I was one of the smallest. I had to stuff my boots full of newspaper so they wouldn't fall off. They were so heavy that unless someone yelled at me to lift up my feet, I just shuffled around as if the boots were bedroom slippers. *This* was how we were going to fight and win a war?

That night we all tried to make improvements to our men's clothes. It was a very domestic scene – hundreds of combat aviators arming themselves with needle and thread and frantically hemming their oversized uniforms. One girl – a pretty blonde who was even smaller than me – took the lining out of her boots and made herself a fur collar with it. (She got in trouble for it later too.) But most of us tried to be more subtle, fixing things so that they fit better and kept us warm.

As we altered our military clothes, I finally got to see the Chief's famous French underwear. It turned out to be a corset, such as fashionable women wore before the Revolution. The Chief set to work taking it apart.

"Don't stare. It's rude," the Chief lisped at me as she ripped it apart at the seams.

Other girls were staring too. The pretty blonde girl giggled and asked, "Does it actually stand up on its own?"

"All by itself," the Chief said.

She propped the corset up to prove it – what was left of it, anyway.

"It holds me up too," the Chief said. "They don't make them like this any more, Blondie, and they never made them like this in the Red Army."

She began to sew the cotton panels to the inside of the man's vest she'd been issued.

Blondie laughed. Then she asked, "Are you hiding diamonds in it?"

The Chief turned towards her, cool and slow and deliberate, and replied, "Like Czar Nicholas II's daughters? Much good it did them."

Blondie shook her head. "You know there are women who show up claiming to be one of those daughters – the Grand Duchess Marie or the Grand

Duchess Anastasia Romanova? They say that in fact they were saved from execution because they had a fortune in diamonds hidden inside their corsets. They say the jewels acted as shields and made the bullets bounce away from their bodies."

The Chief shrugged and said, "Imposters."

This kind of talk always irritated me – partly because Stalin himself had recently forbidden anyone to mention the execution of Czar Nicholas II's family. And partly because – thanks to my father – I knew more than most people about those girls and what happened to them.

But the Chief had my back.

"Such nonsense proves those women are lying," she said. "If someone wants to kill you and your clothes are full of diamonds, he'll shoot you in the head." The Chief's lisping, accented speech was hard to understand, but the blonde girl was listening carefully. "If you can't protect yourself, you need someone else to protect you," the Chief continued. "You know the story of Ivan and the Firebird? When Ivan's jealous brothers slay him, it's the loyal grey wolf who sends for the waters of death and life to revive him." The Chief looked round at us eager young pilots. "We all need a grey wolf beside us."

"That's just a fairy tale!" Blondie exclaimed.

"You can learn from a fairy tale," the Chief said gently. "Look out for each other."

When she'd finished sewing, the Chief turned her vest right-side-out and held it up to show us. The cotton panels sewn inside the vest were completely invisible.

"Now it will hold me up and keep me warm too," the Chief said with satisfaction, then added to the blonde girl, "Let me know if you run out of peroxide, Blondie. I've got a good supply."

Her supply of peroxide was going to last longer than the Chief thought, because we all had to cut our braids off. Someone decided we should get men's haircuts to match our men's uniforms. Some of the girls sobbed when they lost their braids; I wasn't one of them. I wouldn't have cried about my hair in front of the Chief even if I'd felt like it.

After it was cut, the Chief still kept her hair bleached like a starlet's. I wondered what the original colour had been. I thought the Chief looked younger with her hair all shorn – the sides shaved close, with just the forelock on top left a bit longer. It made her look like a boy. A young man – clean-shaven, tough, stout and thuggish.

I saw the Chief checking her face in her compact mirror right after her hair had been cut. I watched her make a conscious decision not to use her precious lipstick.

"Reborn!" the Chief said, and closed the firebird box that held her make-up.

CHAPTER 13

The rail journey to the air force training school at Engels took us over a week. It could have been worse. We were in cars meant for goods, not people, but we had mattresses and blankets. We kept stopping to forage for food – what little there was – or to let more important trains pass us. During the trip, Major Marina Raskova made her way through the train cars, stopping to speak to every one of us.

Major Raskova recognised the Chief. She wrapped her arms around her as if they were sisters, and the Chief returned this embrace stiffly.

"Did you fly all the way from Leningrad?" Major Raskova exclaimed.

"Leningrad is no distance compared to the flights you've made," the Chief pointed out.

They were nothing alike. Major Marina Raskova had a gentle, kind, motherly face and long dark hair pinned at the back of her head. She gave me a warm smile and asked, "Who is this?"

The Chief introduced me. "This is Nastia Nabokova, my only remaining instructor from the Leningrad Youth Aeroclub."

"I've got permission to form three aviation regiments," Major Raskova said. "There will be one regiment of fighters and one of dive-bombers. Those regiments will be equipped with new planes, and when I've finished training all of you I'm going to take command of the dive-bombers. The third regiment will be night-bombers, so we can make best use of all available aircraft."

"I'm guessing the night-bombers will fly Corn-dusters?" the Chief asked. "Carrying bombs under the wings? That's what the air force were going to do with our aeroclub planes when they took them away."

"Yes," Major Raskova replied. "It's a good way to use slow small planes – flying them at night. They'll take a crew of pilot and navigator, so I need navigators as well as ground crew …"

Major Raskova glanced at me. I could tell she was wondering if I'd make a good navigator.

"I will be flying a Yak-1 fighter, and Nastia will be my wingman," the Chief said.

"Everyone wants to fly a fighter, and I need experienced navigators," Major Raskova stated.

"Nastia has already flown in single combat against the Nazi fascists," the Chief said.

Major Raskova looked at me again, with new interest, and demanded, "Tell me about that, Nastia."

The Chief leaned back against the wooden slats of the railway car and folded her arms. She looked as if she wasn't interested. But I knew she was listening closely to my answer.

I also knew I was going to have to add to my story. Not just because I didn't want anyone to know how scared I'd been while the German Messerschmitt fighter was attacking me, but also because I knew I was part of the Chief's plan.

"I couldn't outrace him, so I had to outfly him," I said. "I was over the grounds of the Alexander Palace outside Leningrad ... I didn't have guns of my own, so I lured him to the Red Army gunners in the town of Pushkin, and he fled when he realised they were shooting at him."

It wasn't entirely untrue.

When I'd finished, Major Raskova looked approving. "Well done, Nastia," she said, and then she turned to the Chief and told her, "All right. I won't separate you two. You can fly in the fighter regiment. And Nastia will be your wingman. But behave yourself, will you? I'm going to have to pack two years' worth of training into the next six months."

That was how my disastrous five-minute air chase with the German fighter turned out to be our ticket into the 586th Fighter Aviation Regiment. There, we and thirty-five other women would fly into combat in sleek new Yak-1 fighter planes.

The train rattled over the rails, and the air force training centre got closer with each kilometre. I looked forward to being able to throw my Yak around in the sky as if I were a falcon in flight, and to dive after my prey with machine guns of my own.

PART 4: WINTER, 1942

Engels

CHAPTER 14

Did you know it was the coldest winter ever recorded? *The coldest winter ever recorded.*

The Germans had failed to take Moscow. The cold had stopped them – but they hadn't given up. They were tired and hungry and freezing, but they were willing to wait till spring to start fighting again. And they hadn't given up on Leningrad. My city was still under attack.

Meanwhile, we trained with Marina Raskova at a Soviet Air Force academy in a town called Engels, near the city of Saratov. It was about five hundred kilometres from the battle front. We knew that German fighter planes could reach us in less than an hour if they really wanted to – I thought about it every time I took off. The only thing that stopped them was the cold.

The poor girls who had to check the aircrafts' oil and instruments and adjust the landing gear, and the poor girls who had to learn to load the bombs on the bombers and re-arm the machine guns on the fighters – they had to do it all in temperatures so cold it made their skin stick to the metal they were handling. They'd end up bleeding when they pulled their fingers away. It was so cold some of the girls went around with black spots of frostbite on their cheeks.

Everyone's hands bled with dry, cracked skin, not just the mechanics'. I got chilblains on my fingers just from doing the checks to make sure my plane was in working order. The planes were all mounted on skis instead of wheels during the winter, and we had to prop the skis on pine branches overnight – otherwise they'd freeze to the snow-packed ground before morning.

Once I was in the sky, it was all right. The cramped cockpits of the Yak fighters were heated, so I couldn't complain – not like the open cockpits of the Corn-dusters, which the girls training to be night-bombers had to fly.

I made so many flights as the Chief's wingman that I can't remember them all. But a few of them stand out.

One was a practice flight we made that winter.

In the beginning, as I followed her into the air, it felt like a tour of breathless beauty. The land below us was sparkling white – the snow made it look perfect, unscarred. I could see the smoke rising from the chimneys of Engels and the wide sweep of the frozen Volga River between banks of birch trees – scratches of black and white against clean stretches of snow and ice.

The Chief turned her plane south, in line with the river, heading towards Stalingrad. I followed her around, putting on a burst of speed so I could fly closer to her plane.

She tested me – maybe herself too. She climbed and turned and dived. It took all my focus to keep her in my sight. Finally, the Chief pulled so far ahead of me I lost her white plane against the white landscape.

I made my own plane climb again, trying to get a better view from higher up.

Out of nowhere, a different plane suddenly streaked across my path. It crossed the sky from left to right and made a wide turn to come hurtling back towards me.

The hairs on the back of my neck stood on end. It felt just like that day in the air over the Alexander Palace.

"No, no, no," I whispered to myself. "It must be the Chief in her Yak ..."

But it wasn't. It's hard to tell one aircraft from another in the sky, but I knew the Chief was flying a white plane with spots of shadow here and there. The plane that was circling back to dive at me again wasn't the Chief's white plane. It was gunmetal grey – almost black against the bright blue winter sky.

I tried to keep on flying straight as the other plane swooped back over me again. This time the fighter screamed past me so fast its slipstream buffeted my wings.

I struggled to level out my plane.

Why doesn't he just shoot at me? I wondered. But maybe he'd already won a battle that afternoon and his guns were empty. Maybe he was trying to ram me, to knock me out of the sky ...

I panicked. I forgot about following the Chief. I forgot she was even there, somewhere in that snowy landscape. All I could think about was escaping back to the training base at Engels. All I wanted to do was land safely and sit in my still plane with the canopy open. I wanted to feel the sweet icy wind stinging my cheeks and slicing cracks in my lips.

I turned into a steep climb. My Yak shuddered, almost stalling. Terrible airmanship! I know it! But I was not an amateur – I'd trained dozens of students, and I'd recovered from more stalls than I could count. I wasn't going to crash my plane because of poor flying, even if I was under attack and shaking with terror.

Training and instinct took control of me. I pushed the nose of the aircraft down and gave it full power. My feet moved automatically on the rudder pedals, and my Yak settled back into stable flight.

The other plane was on me again, flying just over my head and a bit behind me. He was so close I could see the hard grey nose of his plane just above my canopy. I cowered, cringing, waiting for the impact.

And then, speeding back towards me so fast that for a second I thought we were going to collide, came a familiar white Yak fighter.

It was the Chief.

Like me, she didn't have live ammunition, but at least there were two of us now.

When the attacking fighter dived away from me again, the Chief dived after it. She made her plane roll and spin so that her opponent couldn't predict her flight path and get the advantage over her that he'd had over me.

For a breathless moment, I watched the two fighter planes dodging and weaving in the sky ahead of me, and they were *beautiful*. They were dancing around each other in the sky, flying *together*—

And that's when I realised that the strange fighter plane was one of ours, and so was its pilot.

It was a Soviet pilot with more experience than me, flying a more powerful and faster plane than my Yak. I hadn't recognised it because sometimes you *can't* see an aircraft's markings when you're in flight – everything moves so fast, and the second the other plane swoops away from you he's too small to see.

I saw the Chief dip her wings in a goodbye wave, and the other pilot dipped his wings back. Just before he flew off, he did a slow, steep turn in the sky ahead of me. The red stars underneath his wings glowed like embers for a moment as the sun picked them out.

The Chief circled back to me. She dipped her wings at me this time, in greeting.

"Looks like he thought he'd have a bit of fun with you, Nastia," the Chief called over the radio. "Mean of him, chasing a rookie like that! Are you all right?"

But I couldn't answer her aloud.

I burned with shame as I dipped my wings in reply, to let her know I was OK.

Then I followed her home.

CHAPTER 15

The Chief landed ahead of me and taxied over to the refuelling station. I parked next to her and watched her lean out of her cockpit to laugh and joke with the mechanics, as if she were nineteen years old like the rest of us.

As the girls began to refuel my own plane, Blondie trundled her Yak up alongside mine and pulled open her canopy. Her cheeks were rosy with the cold and with excitement.

She called to the mechanics, "Hurry up with Nastia's plane, will you? I want to go back up before it gets dark!"

I am not a traitor. But I was still furious with myself for letting the other fighter spook me, and in that moment I really hated both Blondie and the Chief.

The Chief didn't tell anyone about my mistake.

She could have made a real fool of me, but she did not. She didn't even say anything about it to *me*.

So I just had to bear the secret burden of my own stupidity and – for the second time – something that felt like creeping cowardice.

★

I wrote home every week as I'd promised, but I don't know if any of my letters ever reached my parents in Leningrad. The city was still completely blockaded by the German army, and no one could get in or out.

The blockade began on the day we listened to Marina Raskova's radio speech in Moscow in September of 1941, and I do not think it will end before we have won the war.

I got two letters from Leningrad in the spring of 1942, just before our regiment of Yak-1 fighter planes was sent into combat. The letters had been posted in the same mailbag and smuggled out of the blockaded city over the ice road across Lake Ladoga.

The first was from my father, and it was three months old when I got it. He'd written it in January to tell me that my mother had been killed by a bomb. It hit the street while she was walking to work.

It took me several minutes before I could read on. But at last I did, hungry for my father's voice, speaking to me from the ink on the page I held.

My father told me a bit about the Leningrad blockade, how there was no coal and no wood and how everyone in our apartment building had moved all together into four flats on one floor to try to keep warm. He told me how they sat in the cold and dark each night, waiting for the bombing to begin again. Sometimes one of them would starve or freeze to death in the night.

When that happened, they would get rid of the body the next morning and face the new day of cold and hunger. People were eating soup made of boiled shoe leather and wallpaper paste because there was no food.

My father had not been able to go to work since the blockade began, because the Germans had taken over the Alexander Palace to use as their headquarters. So he'd started volunteering at the

Hermitage Museum on the banks of the Neva River in the middle of Leningrad. The curators there were slowly starving to death too, and happy for my father's help. In his letter he told me that the windows of the museum kept being knocked out by exploding shells, and the floors of the exhibition halls were covered with snow and broken glass. My father swept up the glass and dusted the snow from the exhibit cases each morning, and the museum stayed open.

The second letter was more recent, dated within the last month. It was from one of the curators at the Hermitage Museum and said that my father had collapsed on the steps as he left the museum one night.

No one knew whether he'd fallen because of hunger or weakness or cold or a heart attack. No one saw it happen and he didn't get up. By morning he had frozen to death.

I read these letters sitting on the edge of my army camp bed in the barracks at the training base in Engels. Our regiment was about to be sent to its first real wartime assignment, defending the railways and bridges around the city of Saratov. Outside, the snow was melting, turning into slush and mud that made it hard for the planes to take off. The mechanics had removed the skis on some of the Yaks and put the wheels back on, but the ground was so soggy we didn't know which was better. Earlier that week, two of the Corn-dusters had collided in the air during a normal training exercise. Four girls from the night-bomber regiment had been killed in the crash. Everyone was upset.

Now this – my mother and father. *Bombed and frozen to death.*

I sat on the edge of my camp bed, alone, and cried.

CHAPTER 16

The Chief found me.

"Nastia."

She sat down next to me but did not put her arms around me. She just sat there, silent beside me.

After a while, I wiped my eyes and nose and straightened up.

The Chief said, "News from Viktor Nabokov?"

That was my father's name.

I nodded, sniffling. "My father and mother are both dead."

Beside me, I heard the Chief sigh.

"Viktor Nabokov was a good man," she said. "We were comrades in the Revolution. I was young, and he looked after me as a father would, even though he wasn't much older. I don't know why. Perhaps because he knew your mother was going to have a baby soon."

I raised my head to stare at the Chief. She never talked about her past. My father had told me that the Chief had chosen my name, *Anastasia*, meaning rebirth. But he hadn't said why he'd let her do that.

The Chief sat with her arms folded. She wasn't looking at me. She was staring straight ahead, lost in memory. No tears – nothing sentimental. There was no *love* there, or regret. Just respect.

"I have no family," the Chief told me, her voice stiff, "or anyone else special. It keeps my life simple. But I'm sorry about your father, Nastia. I have had a hard life in this new nation of ours. Loyalty means more to me than love."

I was still clutching my father's last letter to me. The Chief gave my hand an awkward pat.

I choked, "Well, now you are stuck with *me*."

"You are my wingman," the Chief said. "I am not stuck with you at all. I *depend* on you."

And I felt a little warmer – and a little braver.

Where does courage come from, and why does it not burn as steadily as loyalty and love? Loyalty and love are the fuel for courage. They never go out.

PART 5: SPRING AND SUMMER, 1942

Saratov

CHAPTER 17

"I'm not ready – not ready – *not ready*."

"Do you know you are speaking aloud?" the Chief asked me mildly.

It was a bright April morning, warm at last, and we were waiting for our Yaks to be fuelled for our first combat flight. We'd moved to our operational base, just ten kilometres from the training centre at Engels. Our new airfield was in a small village across the wide Volga River from the city of Saratov.

The Chief laughed at the expression on my face. I didn't want to get a reputation for muttering to myself.

"Of course you're ready!" she said. "You have twice as many flying hours as that Blondie."

"But she's fearless," I said with envy.

"Ha!" the Chief exclaimed. "She was throwing up in the toilets after supper last night, and it wasn't because she didn't like the cabbage soup.

Everybody's scared. Even those hotshots who flew with the Moscow Aerobatic Team are scared. They show off so people like you can't tell."

I couldn't help laughing.

"You know what your father always used to say before a mission?" the Chief said. "If you're setting out on a long voyage, you're supposed to pretend you're not going anywhere in a hurry. Let's go for a walk around the airfield. Let's find some spring flowers and put a bouquet in Blondie's cockpit!"

★

I was ready, after all.

The order came: "Enemy aircraft heading for Saratov! The Germans are in the air! Twelve *Luftwaffe* bombers and a fighter escort. To your planes! Scramble! Pilots, in the air now!"

As I ran for my Yak, my head was a jumble of thoughts and memories:

My father and mother and my frozen city.

Glass on the museum floor.

The loyal mechanics with their fingers tearing on icy gunmetal.

The buried statue of the girl with the pitcher.

Big Stefan's last salute to me as we said goodbye.

And as my Yak lifted into the sky behind the Chief, I was ready.

I used my old rowing commands as I took off:

"In – three. In – two. In – one. *Go!*"

A dozen of us flew to meet the German bombers.

They were following the Volga River. At first the fighters guarding the bombers were too small to see. But as we sped towards each other, the black spots against the sky became clearer – like a swarm of black ravens in a cloud of black midges.

The midge cloud burst apart as we hurled ourselves into it, and suddenly the black spots became real aircraft. The sky was full of planes. The Luftwaffe bombers of the German air force were easy to see – they were heavy and lumbering and couldn't move smoothly in the sky. They were trying to stay in formation, as if their pilots were huddling together now they were under attack. But I had a hard time telling apart the German and Soviet fighters unless they were close to me. So I stuck like glue to the Chief's tail as she plunged into battle, heading right for the leader of the enemy bombers.

"Come on, Nastia!" the Chief yelled over the radio. "Enjoy this!"

And – I did. Just for a few minutes, my fear turned into exhilaration.

I'd been waiting for this moment all my life.

The Chief was ruthless in the air. She bore down on the leader of the bombers with her machine guns blazing. I flew above her, saving my guns for the Messerschmitt fighters that came screaming in to protect their bomber. The Chief had hit it – she'd knocked out one of its engines. But it didn't fall – it flew on with just one engine running. The Chief made a wide turn to come back after it to finish the job.

Two Messerschmitts followed her, and I went after them. The sky was full of fire and wings.

The Chief's Yak plunged and soared. She circled back towards the bomber she'd hit, going for the other engine. I rose above her. The German bomber glided on, with one engine and one wing in flames. I saw the parachutes of the crew opening below us. They'd be our prisoners now.

I spotted a fighter going down in the distance. For a moment, my heart stopped. One of ours?

Then the Chief's voice came over the radio to reassure me: "That's a Messerschmitt. Blondie's picking them off like birds."

The German planes were scattered now – their organised bombing run had become a mess. The Chief went tearing away to the north, away from the river, chasing a bomber that had been separated from the flock and was flying on to Saratov. I gritted my teeth and tore away after her.

"I'm out of ammunition," the Chief said. "Follow me ..."

That crazy woman dived at the bomber as if she was trying to ram it out of the sky.

She missed. But she'd said to follow her, so I did, throwing my Yak in a dive at the Luftwaffe bomber.

I missed too – but we scared the pilot to bits. He turned too steeply and lost control of his big plane for a moment. That gave us time to soar away and come at him again. We were crows attacking a hawk. And the German bomber did exactly what a hawk would have done: he fled from our territory.

Then, as suddenly as the battle had begun, the sky was clear again.

"Oh, Nastia!" The Chief was elated as we flew back to our base. "You are a warrior, my girl! You are the hope of our nation!"

But I felt like an imposter. I'd hit nothing.

She read my mind and said, "That Blondie will be an ace, yes. But she likes to fly alone, and she'll die alone. I fly with a wingman, and I mean to live."

CHAPTER 18

On the ground, fear was a cancerous thing that ate at you and stopped you from sleeping. But I wasn't worried about air battles any more. On the ground, I worried about other things.

Our forces were being pushed back and back and back, and there was nothing we could do. Our Motherland was burning beneath us. We flew and fought and cried, and flew and fought again.

That summer, Stalin issued Order 227, which forbade us to retreat. The order commanded us: *Not one step back.* Anyone who retreated would be executed. The Germans were pushing us back, but unless we died fighting we would all be shot as traitors.

As pilots, we could fly over the German lines but had to come back to land on a Soviet airfield. Our worst nightmare was that we would be shot down in enemy territory. Anyone who crashed on the wrong side of the front lines and got caught by the Germans would count as a traitor to the Soviet

Union. If we survived as prisoners of the Germans and they ever released us, our own commanders would have to shoot us.

But the enemy was closing in on the city of Stalingrad, trying to get to Moscow by going the long way round. The bombs flew and the city burned, until the flames even licked along the oily surface of the Volga River. The Front grew menacingly closer day by day.

There were two options for a Soviet pilot whose plane was damaged over enemy ground – parachute into the hands of the Germans and risk being shot as a traitor, or try to fly a burning plane back to the safety of our own lines.

Over and over, my comrades chose the second option. They flew burning planes, even if it killed them, rather than risk being taken prisoner by the Germans.

Then, in August 1942, we received an order: "Twenty-eight Luftwaffe bombers coming from Stalingrad! With a fighter escort! All pilots in the air!"

This was to be my last flight with the Chief.

★

I don't know how many Luftwaffe aircraft there were in total that day – fifty at least.

My memory of that battle is like … like trying to recall a whole winter, day by day. You can't remember the separate days, and even if you remember one specific storm, you don't remember each snowflake as it fell. It was like that. Plane after plane came at us, and we fired bullet after bullet back at them. But I don't remember each time I fired at the enemy, or each time I dived away, or each time I felt the jolts of Luftwaffe bullets tearing through my Yak's wings.

I lost the Chief in the battle. It was impossible to keep track of anyone. We defended each other without knowing whom we were defending. One of our planes went down – I did not know whose. Then another.

I do remember the moment when two German fighters collided with each other. The explosion nearly knocked me out of the sky.

And I remember hearing the Chief's radio call to me.

"Nastia, I am out of ammunition," she said, her voice clear and calm.

"*Where are you?*" I screamed.

"Height, two thousand one hundred metres. At the southern edge of the battle. One of the fascist bombers has turned back, and I am going after him," she replied.

"You said you're out of ammunition—"

I cut off, realising what she was going to do. She was going to ram him.

"Wait – *wait!*" I cried. "I'm coming—"

I am no traitor. I have said it before, and I swear it now. And yet, *I left the battle.* I left the battle because I was the Chief's wingman and I had to follow her. And she wasn't running away. She was chasing a bomber four times her size and she had no guns.

I increased the power and lowered the nose of my Yak, trying to get as much speed as I could out of the plane. I thought that if I could overtake the Chief, maybe I could shoot down the bomber before she tried to ram him ...

But I wasn't close enough to do that.

The bomber flew on and on. We flew over long stretches of Stalingrad as it burned. Anti-aircraft guns fired at us from the ground, and I didn't know if those guns belonged to us or to the Germans.

We left the guns behind and flew over the trenches and the wasteland of the Front, into the land occupied by the Germans. In the ruined landscape, there were small fields here and there – yellow with ripe corn and bordered by birch trees with green and trembling leaves.

It looked just like the land on the other side of the line. But we were well into German territory now, and still the Chief chased the enemy bomber, and still I followed her.

I didn't waste my own ammunition, because I was too far behind the bomber to be able to hit anything.

The Chief's Yak was climbing all the time she flew, steadily gaining height. With cool accuracy, she was estimating the angle she'd need to ram the bigger plane. Then, as she moved into position directly above the German bomber, she suddenly pushed her Yak into a screaming dive.

She went for the tail of the bomber. She ploughed into it with the propeller of her Yak. The bomber plunged earthwards, completely disabled by the blow. The Chief's plane descended in a gentle glide, its nose crushed and trailing smoke.

And still I flew after her.

I was still her wingman.

I don't know what I thought I was going to do. Pray for her? Witness her death, anyway.

I'd be her wingman until she stopped flying.

CHAPTER 19

The Chief managed to open the canopy of her damaged plane. Her controls still worked, and she rolled the Yak over so she could fall out of it. The silk of her parachute ballooned below me as I passed overhead.

A Messerschmitt fighter came screaming out of the sky behind me and dived after the Chief. He'd been following me the whole time and, like me, he'd been saving his ammunition.

Now he began firing at the Chief's descending figure beneath the parachute.

He fired and fired until his guns were empty. And then he flew away.

I watched the Chief fall into a field that was green with long grass and bright with wild flowers.

The sky was empty now. I didn't think about where I was or what the consequences might be. I could only think of the Chief. I turned my Yak into a tight descent and landed on the other side of the field.

I scrambled out of the cockpit and into a warm summer breeze. I ran across the field to the fallen parachute.

And she was sitting there among the billows of silk and wild flowers – dazed, bloody, sooty and torn, but still very much alive.

I got down on my knees, facing the Chief, and grabbed her hands, sobbing.

"Shh, shh, Nastia, I'm all right," she told me.

"*How are you all right?*" I cried. "*Are your clothes full of diamonds?*"

"Of course they are," she said.

It took me a moment to realise she wasn't joking.

"They *did* save you!" I cried. "The diamonds in your corset *did* save you!"

"If someone wants to kill you and your clothes are full of diamonds, he'll just shoot you in the head," the Chief insisted. "No – the diamonds just made the deaths of Nicholas II's daughters longer and more frightening. Your father saved me. And today, *you* saved me. Like the grey wolf in the Firebird fairy tale."

Then I whispered, "Which one are you?"

She laughed – a choking, rasping sound – then asked, "Not, *who* are you, but *which one*?"

"You're one of Czar Nicholas II's daughters," I gasped. "One of the Romanov Grand Duchesses. You gave me your sister's name! Or your own! Which one are you?"

"It doesn't matter, does it?" the Chief sighed. "I'm someone else now. I gave new life to an old name when I gave it to you – Anastasia, rebirth. Mother of God, my ribs ache."

I squeezed her hands and asked, "Why didn't you sell them?"

She gave another wheezing laugh. "My ribs?" the Chief said.

"*The diamonds!*" I told her.

"How could I sell them? Where in Russia could I sell them? What use are they to me as jewels? They were my mother's. They're all right as body armour." The Chief looked up at the sky. It was oddly peaceful.

"But you could have left Russia and found another life!" I cried.

"Nastia, my dear, I did find another life," the Chief explained. "And I am going to do that again, now. I am not sure how. Maybe I will be able to creep back across the lines away from the Germans. Maybe a villager will hide me until the war is over. I will fly again, you can be sure. Look for me in the air."

★

I think the Chief was probably the youngest of Czar Nicholas II's daughters.

I think she must have been the Grand Duchess Anastasia Romanova once.

But she isn't any more.

I couldn't take her with me. So I had to let her go.

★

I helped the Chief bundle up the parachute. It would keep her warm. She might be able to trade it if she found someone willing to give her shelter.

She *might* be able to trade a diamond or two.

I gave her my matches and my knife and my water bottle and my compass. I gave her my china pencil. That was all she would let me give her. Then she helped me turn my Yak around, one of us guiding each wing, so I could take off into the wind.

"Use the short field take-off technique," the Chief told me. "The field may be mined. Be careful! Ah, wait ..."

She dug into the breast pocket of her blouse and pulled out a cigarette and matches. "Pretend you're not going anywhere in a hurry."

We shared the cigarette without speaking. My hands trembled – hers did not. When the last of the ash fell away, she put her hand on my arm and pushed me towards the plane.

"All set, Nastia?" the Chief asked. "After the war is over, when they dig up that bronze girl with a pitcher in the Catherine Park, rub her foot for luck again and give her my greetings."

I gave a choking laugh.

After I climbed into my Yak's cockpit, I could not see the instrument panel because my eyes were so blurred with tears. The Chief had already started walking away, her back to me. Reborn.

CHAPTER 20

You may judge for yourself whether I endangered my Motherland or my comrades. I will wait for the decision of this tribunal, and the sentence. But I am no traitor.

I took off blindly from that field in German territory.

In the air, I had to wipe my eyes and pull myself together so I could see to fly. I had to work out my position above the Volga River so I could find my way home.

And there were more Messerschmitts in the sky ahead of me.

For a moment, I was overcome with exhaustion. Wouldn't it just be easier to let them shoot me down and get it over with?

"*I gave new life to an old name when I gave it to you – Anastasia, rebirth.*" Those were the Chief's words.

No. I'd never give up that easily. I flew to meet the Messerschmitts.

I still had ammunition in my guns. I began to fire.

And suddenly, off to my right but not where I was aiming, one of the Messerschmitts exploded in flames. I veered towards the burning plane, hoping my remaining enemies wouldn't follow, and glanced up through my clear canopy. Another Soviet fighter was above me in the sky. The sunlight gleamed for a moment on the red stars beneath its wings and then glanced away.

The other plane wasn't a Yak, so it wasn't anyone from my regiment. It was a stranger from another regiment who'd seen a comrade in trouble and had come to join the battle.

Now he was in trouble too, so I turned back to defend him.

But he didn't fly the way the Chief flew. He didn't act as a leader for me to follow. He was fighting his own battle, engaging one of the Messerschmitts and leaving me to deal with the other. We soared and plunged in parallel, each protecting the other by attacking an individual enemy.

I managed to shoot the tail off the German plane I was chasing. As the enemy fighter fell, I saw the now-familiar bloom of a parachute unfold beneath me.

I had destroyed my first Messerschmitt.

There was one German fighter left.

The stranger was still flying his Soviet plane parallel to me. I was sure we could take down this last Messerschmitt if we worked together.

"Stay on him!" I yelled over the radio. "We'll fire together! In – three. In – two. In – one – *FIRE!*"

The aircraft ahead of us became a ball of black smoke and red flame. If I kept going, I would fly right into the explosion. I turned so fast I felt my Yak shudder on the edge of a stall.

"*Hold her up!*" I yelled. I was encouraging myself out loud again.

I levelled out as the Messerschmitt plummeted beneath me. We'd done it. And then I was alone in the sky with the Soviet aircraft.

I dipped my wings at him. He dipped his wings in a friendly wave back at me and circled around to fly by my side.

"Thanks, Nastia," he said over the radio.

My mouth dropped open. How could the other pilot *possibly* know who I was in the air? I looked over at his plane, flying wingtip to wingtip with me.

I couldn't see his face – all I could see was a helmeted head in the cockpit. He waved at me with frantic excitement.

"I'd know that command anywhere!" came his voice. "We rowed together in Leningrad, remember? I was your stroke!"

"*Big Stefan!*" I realised. I laughed aloud, delighted and astonished. "You're still alive!"

"I'm based on the edge of Stalingrad," he told me.

"I'm at Saratov!"

"Thanks for coming to my rescue," he said. "I was worried for a moment ..."

"Not one step back!" I reminded him.

Big Stefan laughed. "You are still the revolutionary's daughter!"

For another thirty seconds, we flew side by side.

"I'm low on fuel," I said. "I have to re-join my regiment."

"I do too," Big Stefan replied.

Below us, the blue of the sky was reflected in the Volga River, and the outline of our planes was reflected in the blue. On either side of the river were fields of sunflowers. For a moment, it was like flying in peacetime: like pretending you're not in a hurry before you set out on a long journey.

Then we had to part.

"See you in the sky another time, Nastia," Big Stefan called to me.

"I hope so!" I cried. "Take care!"

Just before Big Stefan turned away, he saluted me. Then, with a flash of sun on the red stars beneath his wings, he was gone.

The Chief. Big Stefan. I knew I would probably never see them again.

I flew on anyway.

Do with me what you will ...

AUTHOR'S NOTE

According to DNA evidence, Anastasia Romanova and her entire family died together in the terrible execution of the last Russian Czar in 1917. But that proof hasn't stopped people from wondering what might have happened if Anastasia had survived. Over the last century, impostors have turned up pretending to be one or another of the murdered Romanovs, and they have inspired many fictional accounts of Anastasia's survival.

As an author, I like to point out the places where fact and fiction meet, and where they go in different directions – just so the reader is aware that my story *is* only a story, and *not* the truth.

The diamonds were real. Many rich Russians fled with their jewels to other cities in Europe because of the Revolution. I have no doubt Czar Nicholas II's family would have done the same if they'd been able. They really did hide a small fortune in jewels in their underwear, in the hope that the family would be able to escape and make a new life for themselves. The murder of Nicholas II's children became a real massacre because the jewels turned their underwear into bullet-proof vests. Shooting at the children didn't kill them, so the executioners resorted to slashing at them with bayonets.

The name of the man who drove the getaway truck that carried the bodies is known, and he was not Nastia's father. His name was Pyotr Zakharovich Yermakov, and his role in the execution is described by Yakov Yurovsky, the chief executioner, in his official account of what happened that night in July 1918. You can read that account yourself on the Alexander Palace website.

Yurovsky lived for another twenty years. He married, had a son and a daughter, and became the director of a science museum. I'd love to say that this is where I got the idea for Nastia's father's job, but it isn't – I didn't find out about Yurovsky's museum work until *after* I'd written *Firebird*. Sometimes truth is as strange as fiction.

Soviet women who fought in the Second World War have given many personal accounts of their wartime experiences, and I used a number of these as inspiration for Nastia's story. The young spy who rubbed salt into her baby's skin was Maria Timofeevna Savitskaya-Radiukevitch, as told in Svetlana Alexievich's wonderful book *The Unwomanly Face of War* (but it happened in the Second World War, not during the Russian Civil War).

For Nastia's experience of the first day of the war, I put together two stories: tail-gunner Antonina Khokhlova-Dubkova's trip to the recruitment office with her rowing team, and fighter pilot Olga Yakovleva's memory of hearing an announcement on public loudspeakers while she was sunbathing by the Miass River.

For Nastia's escape from Leningrad, I was inspired by dive-bomber pilot Maria Dolina's account of having to evacuate and burn her own aeroclub. And for the time that Nastia spends in Moscow before she joins Marina Raskova's regiments, I was influenced by armourer Irina Lunyova-Favorskaya's account of digging defensive ditches in her underwear.

I found these interviews in Anna Noggle's *A Dance with Death: Soviet Airwomen in World War II* and Kazimiera Janina Cottam's *Women in Air War: The Eastern Front of World War II*.

There was a real incident similar to the one where the Soviet plane swoops down on Nastia and pretends to attack her while she's training. It happened when the 588th Night-Bomber Regiment were on their way to their first operational air base. A group of male fighter pilots had been sent to escort the young women of the regiment and decided to have some fun with them, but the female air crews scattered in every direction, thinking they were under attack. They were so badly shaken by the joke that they had to rebuild their confidence by spending another two weeks training at their new base. Only then were they allowed to fly their first wartime combat missions.

I wrote the radio broadcasts in *Firebird* myself, but I didn't make up their content. The announcer's speech in Chapter 10 is based on Josef Stalin's first wartime radio broadcast to the nation on 3 July 1941. Marina Raskova's radio broadcast in *Firebird* is loosely based on a speech she made at a Women's Antifascist Meeting on 8 September 1941. An account of the real speech is given in a book about Marina Raskova's life by Russian writer Galina Markova.

Marina Raskova, like Anastasia Romanova, was a real person. Marina broke records with her aviation trips across the Soviet Union before the Second World War and was adored as a heroine by young pilots all across the country. Her feats even achieved international fame at the time. She personally organised the three women's aviation regiments that fought and flew for the Soviet Union in the Second World War.

Like the speeches and the events of Nastia's life, most of the setting and action of my story is invented but based on reality. The Leningrad Youth Aeroclub and the First Neva Rowing Club don't exist, but they're very similar to thousands of real youth clubs in the Soviet Union of the 1930s. Soviet girls and boys at that time were given equal educations, and they were all required to join paramilitary clubs for teens (much like the Combined Cadet Force or Air Cadets in the United Kingdom today).

One final incredible detail I want to share is about the way the Chief rams her aircraft into the German plane at the end of *Firebird*. This is based on a strategy called *taran*, which was used as a desperate measure by Russian pilots when they'd run out of ammunition or fuel. A *taran*, or ramming attack, was not a suicide move. There were different ways in which you could ram an enemy aircraft and survive. One Soviet woman, Yekaterina Ivanovna Zelenko, is known to have carried out a successful *taran* attack against a German aircraft in the Second World War. Witnesses said that she was still in control of her own plane after the attack, but was shot down and killed by another German fighter.

For the past few years, I've been researching all the material that's available in English about the amazing women who fought in air combat for the Soviet Union in the Second World War. At the same time, I've been fascinated by the story of Czar Nicholas II's children and of the many women who have insisted they were Anastasia Romanova during the last century. My daughter Sara, a film student, has joined me in this, doing her own research into the theatrical and media productions inspired by Anastasia's story and sharing her finds with me.

It has been a joy to be able to pull all these interests together into my own work of fiction. Playing with history's "what-ifs" is one of a novelist's greatest pleasures.

Our books are tested
for children and young people by
children and young people.

Thanks to everyone who consulted on
a manuscript for their time and effort in
helping us to make our books better
for our readers.